Straight Curve

Drama, Emotion, Humour and Hope

Ruthvik

ISBN 979-8-89002-938-6

Disclaimer

The content in this book is purely fictional and imaginary. If you find any correlation with real life, it is purely coincidental because I only copied in exams. Vocabulary, Names of the characters, References to Bollywood movies and non-English language words are all ~~copied~~ inspired. The stories, the morals, the P.S., the titles, the thought in the chapters, the timelines, the nonsense (if any) and the grammatical mistakes are all something that is of my own.

Table of Contents

Preface

I never thought I will write a Preface owing to two reasons. One, my language skills were so bad I never even wrote a leave letter without grammatical mistakes. I was beaten up more by teachers for grammatical mistakes than for being absent. So, a '**Preface**' was out of reach. Two, I thought Preface and Prefix were the same. Whenever I heard the word '**Preface**' I thought people were referring to the word '**Prefix**' but with an accent.

So, when a good friend of mine asked if I was writing a Preface for the book, I wondered why I would need to add Mr./Ms./Dr. to the title of the book. It would end up as **Mr. Straight Curve** or **Ms. Straight Curve** which made no sense.

It was not until I saw her bewildered expression that I realized I was completely off the mark. Thanks to Google, not only did I understand what a Preface was, but I also found some great prefaces to copy over. However, I soon realized that Prefaces are like love letters. Both are meant to express and not impress. So, here I am, writing my Preface.

Right from my childhood, waiting at the traffic signal, standing in the queue at the grocery store, or watching non-skippable ads on YouTube have been opportunities for my imagination to run wild. This book is a culmination of such imaginations coming together in the form of short stories with little emotion, some drama, a few twists, and a lot of hope, just like our lives.

If any line in the book reminds you of an old friend or if any paragraph makes you nostalgic in a good way or if any chapter makes you smile a little, the book and the author will feel extremely happy.

If you know me and are reading this book, thanks for all the patience, support, and trust. If you do not know me and are still reading this book, I could not thank you more for all the love. If I ever get to meet you someday, I will hug you and say, "Thank you." So, if one day, a stranger hugs you out of the blue with a blue shirt on (I love blue shirts), the chances of it being me are extremely high.

Hope you like it and wish to meet you again on the last page!

A Few People to Thank!

<u>**Family:**</u>

My parents, C Suprasanna Devi and R Ramchander Rao met at a bus stop, fell in love, fought hard with obstacles, and got married. 37 years later, they still love each other and have showered unquantifiable love towards me and my brother. What better platform than this book to share a couple of anecdotes and thank them?

When I was 4 feet tall, I joined swimming classes, and on the 3rd day adrenaline kicked in, and I jumped into 7 feet. It did not take me more than 4 seconds to realize that I'm only left with 40 seconds in my life as I was drowning. Within 5 seconds, a middle-aged man who does not know swimming jumps into the pool and somehow gets me out of the pool. It is my dad and if required, he would have jumped into the ocean for me.

I failed 8th grade, and I was afraid of how my mom would react. All that she told me was, it is fine as things happen. We know what you are, and we do not define our love for the grades you get. I thought I would cry that day for being beaten up, but I cried for the love showered. Glad I failed 8th grade. There were times I did not love myself enough but there was never a time when my parents did not love me.

And there is another person without whom I cease to exist. It is my younger brother, (Indraneel, Jixu). I might become captain of the Indian Cricket Team if I tried hard, but I can never match the amount of love showered by my brother towards me.

I was in 4ᵗʰ grade when I was attacked by a few dogs and I thought I will at least have 4 scars. But, my brother, in 1ˢᵗ grade back then, who was also scared of dogs, comes in, covers me up, and tries dodging them. Since then, he kept covering me whenever life gave me a tough time. There were times when I did not feel confident about myself, but there was never a time when my brother didn't feel confident about me.

Thank you, Mom, Dad, and Jixu for being the support pillars of my life. All that I am today is because of you and someday I will make you all proud. If given a chance to choose a family for my next birth (if it exists), I'd choose the same people in the same order.

Thank you, Familia!

<u>**Friends:**</u>

This piece of work wouldn't have reached your hands if not for a few people.

Prakhar Agarwal: The best critic I could ever ask. If not for him, I would have published the book with all blank pages. He might not even put in so much effort for his own book too. Thanks for all the effort in reviewing each and every word in the book and sharing some honest feedback. He currently works for the Government of India and is the most eligible bachelor in his room.

Neha Agarwal: *"If had friends great, memories great have you"* would have been the sentences in the book with my English standards. But, with all the efforts of reviewing she has put in, sentences like the above have become **"If you have great friends, you will have great memories"**. Thanks Neha for all the support and help. She currently works as a product manager in an MNC and aspires to write a book one day (Hope she doesn't ask me to review her work).

When I started writing, I wasn't sure about the topics I want to write pages except for one; the Thank you page.

It is fine to not know people who don't like/love you, but it is important to know the people who like/love you. And I have been fortunate to have a few such great human beings in my life whose presence has been priceless. If there's anything I am proud of, it is the friendships I've earned. Only when I started listing down the people, I realized how blessed I am. Here are a few such wonderful people I thank from the bottom of my heart.

Kaushik, Ananth, Mohan, Rahul, Kushal, Ravi Teja, Hiranya, Manikanta, Bharat, Veeranjineyulu, Sasanka, Santosh, Satya, Tarun, Varshneya, Sabi, Praveen, Srinivas, Saikumar, Anusha, Vamshi, Chakrapani, Murali, Joseph, Srivardhan, Anurag, Sandeep, Pratik, Nabin, Anish, Riya, Mohit, Arjun, Joel, Marzook, Akanksha, Sajil, Shriram, Vishnu, Vinutna, Abhishek, Bhargav, Ahana, Prashant, Dinesh, Sainath, Charan, Priyanka, Bharadwaj and Ashwini.

The list has been a bit long and I feel fortunate for the same.

<u>**Professors:**</u>

Dr. Padmini Cheerla (Associate Prof., Associate Dean (Student Affairs) at Vardhaman College of Engineering, Hyderabad)

I'd like to take this opportunity to thank her for all the belief she had in me when I even doubted myself. In the last few years, because of post-graduation and work, I gave a lot of presentations. But the first presentation I ever gave was on her subject, back in 2012. I was nervous, couldn't speak a word and almost gave up on presentations. But she encouraged and kept motivating me.

"Thank you, Ma'am, for being such a positive influence in my life. I will never forget the life lessons I picked up from you and it truly was a blessing being your student. Thank you for being kind and empathetic."

P. Vigneswara Ilavarasan (Professor - IIT Delhi; Social Media; Digital Economy; Business/Market Research; Impact Assessment; ICTD; Data Analysis)

Just before I joined the MBA, a friend of mine told me that the professors at IIT are very tough and serious. But then I came across Prof P. Vigneswara Ilavarasan, one of the coolest professors I ever met during my academic stint.

Never did I or any of the students in his class return back without a little laughter. Such was his humor and impact on the class. Even after 6 years of my post-graduation, a lot of my friends still recall how he made us comfortable during the admission and interview process.

Thank you, Sir, for making us understand how important it is to not take life very seriously, and how important it is to stand for what we believe. Thank you so much for caring about us beyond what your profession requires.

<u>Mentors:</u>

Big thanks to CV Ramanuja Chary, Ashwini, Aditi, Phalguna, Manasa, Harini, Vivek & Akhil for guiding me.

1

Dhoni Finishes off in Style

Around 1:30 PM, 08th Jun 1999, Tuesday, just after the lunch break, The day of the Ind vs. Pak World Cup Cricket Match: I was 7 years old and I knew no more than my parents and Ruchi (my friend) from school. I had zero to no interest in the class and was busy talking to Ruchi. And, all that I prayed to god was for the school to be over soon. And, all of a sudden, in comes the peon with notice. He gave it to the teacher, and she read my name and asked me to take my bag and leave the class. I thought they suspended me for talking to Ruchi. But only then I realized that my father came to take me back home half-day. I bid goodbye to Ruchi and left. There's no better feeling than your parents coming to school and taking you back home half-day. It's like an official bunk. During the drive back home, I asked him the reason and he told me about the world cup match India is playing against Pakistan. Dumb me thought, my father, is making me play a world cup match. I was wondering how many days it will take and was feeling sad for Ruchi for missing me. Note that, I didn't even ask my dad what a world cup was, or what sport it was. Only after going back home, I realized he just brought me back home to watch it. Poor Ruchi, she missed the chance of missing me.

All that I knew about cricket was that my dad likes cricket. For the first time, my mom didn't deny me from watching television citing eye strain. Instead, the rule was that I will have to watch Cricket and not the cartoon. I felt betrayed by my mother for the first time. When I watched cricket for the first time, all I noticed was a few people wearing colourful t-shirts and they were trying to harm one person standing in the middle by throwing a ball at him. Poor lad is trying to protect himself with a piece of wood and was running at random. Cricket seemed more of harassment and less of a game. In the meanwhile, all of my dad's friends started coming in. I thought, my dad is organizing a house party for everyone to witness the harassment.

Everyone found me cute and squeezed my cheeks in between the overs. All of them were having alcohol, and I was given juice. Not a bad deal for a 7-year-old though. And, all of us enjoyed our respective drinks. Our house looked like a mini cricket stadium. There was no room for a 7-year-old to run around. But, on the contrary, my dad was enjoying it like never before. It was an eventful day.

12th Jun 1999, Saturday, Evening: We were knocked out of the world cup. My dad was very upset and he told me, *"We last won a world cup back in 1983, and we didn't have access to televisions back then. All that we had was the radio and it was one of the happiest days of my life. Hopefully, we will win a world cup again."*

With all my brain, I visualized how my dad would've felt on the night of the 1983 world cup final. All that I could visualize was him being ecstatic and joyous. But only visualizing didn't satisfy my soul. I wanted to watch my dad re-live the moment again. Since then, I wanted India to win the world cup again and It became my dream.

By 2003, I was as much a cricket fan as my dad, and we almost made it. But you know what happened. The Australians were ruthless. I cried a river post the result. My dad consoled me saying, ***It's a cricket match, we will win someday, and we will lose someday.*** Little did he know about my dream being shattered!

I thought the 2007 50-over world cup would be one step better. But we were back at square one. (Note, that my dad doesn't like T20 cricket. So, I couldn't convince him to watch it). Years passed on; Captains and coaches changed. A few years later, in 2011, we had a world cup happening in India. I had no hopes, but, somewhere at the back of my mind, I knew there was a chance.

In the Quarters, we defeated the Australians. Slowly, my dad started gaining interest in the progress. And, it was semis. We got the better of Pakistan. And, my dad was tenser than me during the match.

And, finally, it was D-day. Just like in 1999, my dad called all his friends. Felt like a Déjà vu of 1999. The only change was they didn't find me cute this time. And, all of my dad's friends were having alcohol again and offered me juice just like the last time. It didn't seem fair this time. I thought of snatching a beer from one of them and taking a sip. But my mom doesn't know about my drinking habits and when I looked at my mom, she was already looking at me to see if I am picking up the beer bottle. Luckily, I didn't.

Dhoni was making on-field strategies to get a wicket and I was making off-field strategies to get the beer. After a couple of overs, both Dhoni and I succeeded. With utmost caution, I was sipping coke (I mean beer in the coke tin). This time, there was a lot of room for an 18-year-old to run around. But I choose not to. I was just watching my dad enjoy the moment. After a few hours, it was all anxiety and excitement.

And, the final moments have arrived. India needed 6 runs with Kulasekara charging in. Everyone in the house, or probably everyone in the country had their eyes on Dhoni and I had my eyes on my dad. A few seconds later, my dad jumped for joy, and he whistled. And, in parallel, I heard, Ravi Shastri's commentary, ***"Dhoni finishes off in style."*** Time stopped around me and I missed watching Dhoni hit six live. But I made sure to see my dad celebrating. It was an emotional moment for every cricket fan in the country, and so was it for me. Just that the reasons were a little different. My dream of watching my dad re-live the moment of India winning the world cup finally came true. It was a dream for 12 years, and I couldn't control my tears. My dad hugged me and said the same thing he said back in 2003, ***"It's a cricket match, we will win someday, and we will lose someday."***

Little did my father know about the dream of a 7-year-old kid! And, likewise, little did MS Dhoni know the dream he fulfilled.

Thank you, Mahi, for fulfilling a nations and a son's dream at once. On that day, I've realized one thing. Like SRK said, 'Kehte hain agar kisi cheez ko dil se chaho … to poori kainath use tumse milane ki koshish mein lag jaati hai.'

P.S: Sapne har baar khud ke kushi se poore nahi hote hain, kabhi sapne apno ke kushi se bhi poore hote hain!

Moral of the Story: Keep dreaming for others too. There's joy second to none when they get fulfilled.

Mahendra Singh Dhoni, collecting tickets to fulfilling dreams.

2

Nadaan Parinde Ghar Aaja

05:15 PM, 29th Sep 2011, Thursday, Hyderabad, in a nearby Park: I was taking a stroll in the park and was lost in thoughts. I was in under-graduation and it was one of those days which didn't go well. I spent the first half of the day standing outside of the class as a punishment for answering when someone asked me a question *(I was whispering answers to my friend in an exam)*. And, I spent the second half too outside the class as a punishment for not answering when someone asked me a question *(I was silent when my teacher asked me a question in Viva)*. For the entire day, all that I did was stand outside. I thought to myself, *"Such an outstanding student"*

I came back to reality and realized, I already walked 7 rounds and felt it to be more than enough for the day. Just then I saw Ramya *(who stays in my neighbourhood and I liked her very much)* entering the park. My last round became the first one *(Fitness is my passion)*. We both are a pair together is what my friends think, we both are future husband and wife is what I think, we both are just friends is what she thinks and we both are siblings is what her father thinks.

I greeted her, and we both started walking. After a few minutes, she asked me if I could accompany her to the movie *'Rockstar'* releasing the next day. Is there anyone who'd decline to go to a movie with their crush? I had zero knowledge of Bollywood movies and the only Hindi language movie I watched was *'Anaconda (Dubbed in Hindi)'* when my school took us as a part of recreational activity. To date, I couldn't figure out how is watching Anaconda a recreational activity.

With a poker face, I replied, ***"Yah! I too was waiting for the release of Rockstar."*** She had a big smile and I responded similarly. Before I collapsed with tiredness, it was sunset, and we headed back home. I spent the next few hours researching the cast and crew of the movie.

07:17 AM, 30th Sep 2011, Friday, Hyderabad, In a Neatly Organized Bedroom, 'Tringgg Tringgg': It was just the 6th alarm and I was only 10% awake. I was still dreaming about my marriage with Ramya. I'm sure Ramya must be dreaming the same too. (But with Ranbir Kapoor). But who cares? I'm the hero of my dreams.

And, in the meanwhile, the alarm rang for the 7th time, and I was 50% awake now. With great difficulty, I looked into the other room and noticed my father giving me glances filled with anger for all the alarms missed. I was 100% awake now. A single stare from my father did what 7 alarms couldn't. I got ready in a jiffy, told my parents that I have an important class to attend, and told my friends that I have an important family function to attend I left for the theatre to meet Ramya. She brought the tickets for us and I bought some love for her.

10:20 AM, Same Day, IMAX Theatre, Rows C-17, and C-18: I didn't understand the movie as I was very bad at

Hindi. There were subtitles, but they were moving fast and I couldn't concentrate. I gave up on and decided to look at Ramya and admire her. And, in parallel, I heard, *'Nadaan Parinde Ghar Aaja'* for the first time. Visuals and lyrics didn't matter to me (As I was busy admiring Ramya) but the music sounded great (Courtesy: ARR). A couple of hours later, the movie ended, Ramya had the joy of admiring Ranbir Kapoor and I had the joy of admiring her. Post the movie, we went back home. Just as I reached, I passed orders to my brother to turn the geyser on, threw clothes as far as I could for my mom to pick up, and had a nice shower and a great dinner. Ah! Felt like the king of the house.

07:15 AM, 21ˢᵗ Jan 2016, (Half a decade later), Thursday, Bengaluru, Completely Messed Bedroom, 'Tringgg Tringgg': It was the 6ᵗʰ alarm and I was only half-awake. A lot of things changed in the 5 years, but the old habit of not waking up to alarms didn't. As they say, *'Old habits die hard.'* But, before the 7ᵗʰ alarm rang, I woke up and my subconscious memory kept telling me I'd be late to work if I don't wake up in the next few seconds. It was wrong as I was already late by then.

In Parallel, I happened to listen to *'Nadaan Parinde Ghar Aaja'* played on YouTube by my roommate. But this time I don't have Ramya by my side as we broke up, but hearing this song took me back to the old times. Visuals (Didn't matter to me as I was rushing to get ready for work), Lyrics (Hit me hard and I gave up on getting ready for office) and music still sounded great (Courtesy: ARR).

I visualized my younger self from 2011 and thought, **"How much has my life changed."** I've seen some major changes between the two *'Nadaan Parinde Ghar Aaja'* songs heard over a gap of 5 years.

It's been a few years since I left home for education and work. But it feels like I've been away from home for two decades now. At some point in time, all of us would've missed home and felt homesick. I too was one of them.

A few love Diwali, a few Ramadan, and a few Christmases. But, we, the people staying away from home, love festivals without any religious barrier. All that we want is to go back home and spend some time with family/friends. Long weekends are the ones when we and the travel agents get rich. We get rich from the memories we earn during our home visits, and the travel agents get rich from the money we pay them for the tickets.

To get leave to go back home, I faked attending marriage alliances, pretended to be sick, and killed my grandfather multiple times. Hope he forgives me from heaven. After all, I killed him after his death only to spend time with his daughter and son-in-law. As they say, everything is fair in love and war. And, over the years, owing to academics and careers, we all kept fighting wars only to spend some time with loved ones back home.

Travelling in a sleeper class with waitlisted ticket felt more luxurious than a confirmed 1AC seat while returning.

Days pass like minutes when we visit home, and seconds pass like years when we are away. Textbooks taught us the theory of life while staying away from home taught us the practical's of life.

From being careless to becoming conscious

From taking pocket money from parents to managing own expenses

From being consoled by parents for the slightest inconvenience to handling heartbreaks by self

From fighting with siblings even for small things to helping each other in the struggles of life

From getting food served in bed by parents to cooking food for self

From meeting friends and planning on a vacation to planning to meet friends only on vacation

From complaining about home-made food to craving home-made food

From lying to your parents to see your friends, to lying to your boss to see your parents

From crying while leaving home for first time, to managing a smile every time you leave home

From being the king/queen of your world to adjusting to the world around you

A quote from the author of this book; *If you lived at home, you'll only know how to live at your home. But, if you lived away from home, you'll know how to live anywhere in the world*.

Cheers to everyone for handling the highs and lows during the journey. Sometimes, we come out of the home to earn and we spend it only to go back home to spend time with our loved ones. Every time, we see our loved ones, our happiness becomes multi-folds and our sorrows one-tenth.

P.S: Chota ho yah badaa, multi floor yah single floor, duniya ke iss paar, yah uss paar. Ghar pyara hota hain, kyu ki woh hamaara hota hai. Zindagi guzarne ke liye ghar se jaana mazboori hai, par, zindagi kushi se guzarne ke liye ghar waapas aana bhi zaroori hain.

09:45 AM, Same Day, *Homesickness kicks in*: Just realized, I spent two hours thinking about all this and I couldn't resist anymore as I badly want to go back home. I rang up my boss, killed my grandfather again, applied for planned sick leaves for 4 days, and logged on to the IRCTC portal to book a train ticket to go back home.

3

Kabhi Khushi Kabhi Gham

06:17 AM, 07th Dec 2017, Thursday, Mumbai, Bedroom, Phone rings (*you made me a believer a, you made me a believer*): I usually stay awake all night and sleep during the day. Everyone except my boss knows about my sleeping cycle. Glad he did not know about it, else, he would have tagged me in night shifts.

So, the phone ring felt like a dream, and I ignored it as long as I can. The decibels of the ring and my irritation increased with every second. After 10 seconds, I woke up and thought to myself; **"Even if it's my girlfriend I will not pick up the call"** (I don't have a girlfriend though). But then it was my boss, so I picked up. *(If your boss is calling you so early in the day, it's only for two things. Either you have screwed something up at work or he/she wants you to work on some important task ASAP.)*

I was curious about what it was with me. My boss started with, *"Hey Kaushik, you are an absolute genius"* (Oh, so, this is for the second one and he wants me to do some task). I kept listening to him and after 15 seconds of praising me, he says, *"Hey Kaushik, I need you to be in the office by 07:15 AM buddy, there is an important deliverable that must be worked on ASAP. I believe in you buddy."* I thought, *"Don't go by my ringtone. I just liked the song and kept it as my ringtone."*

With no option left, I replied, *"Sure."* He acknowledged and disconnected the call. I got up from the bed, walked to the balcony, and saw a few birds chirping. I never saw them on our balcony, and they never saw me either as we had issues with time zones as I sleep late and they come early in the morning. I took a picture of them and updated a story on Instagram with the caption *'Mornings are Beautiful.'* I was just trying to make the most of my morning and with no delay, I got ready and left for work.

07:27 AM, Same Day, and Workplace: I reached the office and opened the logbook to enter my details at the reception, and as expected I was the first one at work. Right from my schooling, I always prayed to the almighty to help me come first. But I never wanted to come first to work. (Guess my prayers were misunderstood). Anyway, I walked into the lift, pressed 8, and started cursing my boss. 7 seconds later, I reached the 8th floor, 7 minutes later, I reached my cubicle and 70 minutes later, I finally stopped cursing him

09:08 PM, Same Night, Workplace, 7 minutes to the last office shuttle: The quick ask of my boss took the entire day. I shut the laptop and started packing my bag and while I was doing so, I saw *Mohan*, a colleague of mine still working and felt pity for him as I was sure he would miss the shuttle. I laughed at his situation and ran to catch the shuttle. I reached the shuttle just a minute away from 09:15 PM.

I found a nice window seat in the empty bus and plugged in my earphones. After 4 songs from the movie Tamasha, I was still in the same place as the traffic didn't let the bus move an inch. (Why did I even run then? I would've easily made it even if I walked). I then saw *Mohan* walking into the bus. He reciprocated me with the same laugh I gave him some time ago (Karma).

After 20 minutes, and a repeat of those 4 songs, traffic eased and I reached home. And, just as I enter, I saw, *Ananth*, a roommate of mine washing his car. It was weird as I never watched him do so because he has never done that.

If he feels cold half-way through the night, he will not reduce the fan speed; instead, he'll take a Paracetamol in the morning once he gets sick. That lazy he is and with all my curiosity, I asked him what he is up to. With his smile matching the levels of my curiosity, he replied, ***"I have a breakfast date tomorrow."***

"We skip breakfast only to get a little more sleep and here you are, planning for a breakfast date" was what I wanted to say but I ended up saying, ***"Good luck mate!"*** and went to my room and within a few minutes, I fell asleep.

06:08 AM, 08th **Dec 2017, Friday, Bedroom, "Kaho Na Pyaar Hai" plays in the background:** Just like the previous day, the sound kept increasing and a couple of stanzas later, I woke up to see where it was coming from. It took me 2 half-opened eyes, 1 full minute, and 3 confused glances across the room to realize *Ananth* playing it while getting ready for his date.

Ignoring it, I checked my phone and saw a WhatsApp notification from my boss, *"Hey Kaushik, I need you to be in the office by 07:15 AM buddy, there's an important deliverable that has to be worked on ASAP. I believe in you buddy."* I thought to myself, *"Does he have this sentence copied? He's using it as-is every time."* I too repeated the reply from the previous day, and as a daily routine, I greeted the birds (we both looked at each other with some familiarity now) and got ready to work.

07:45 AM, Same Day, and Workplace: Just like the previous day, I opened the logbook and to my surprise, I wasn't the first one. For the first time ever, I felt happy for not being the first one. I entered the details, took the lift, pressed 8, and started cursing my boss, 7 seconds later I reached the 8th floor, and 7 minutes later I reached the cubicle and continued to curse him for 35 minutes with working in parallel. Suddenly, I felt someone tapping on my shoulder and with the mood, I was in, I didn't feel any happier and all of it showed on my face when I turned around. I saw **Chitra** with a helpless look and it didn't take much time for me to put up a smiling face. I replied, *"Hey, Hi Tell me, how can I help you?"*

And, her response was sweet, *"Hi, I am Chitra, and I'm a fresher staffed on the same project as yours. I am new to the project and our boss asked me to take your help on C language."* I thought to myself, *"My boss is a gem of a guy."*

I know who she was. Because Chitra was from Chennai and for me, she was the most beautiful girl on our floor and she has been my office crush since the time she joined, but I never had the courage or opportunity to approach and talk to her. With inspiration from SRK's acting, I pretended to not know her and I continued. *"Hey Sure, I will help you out. I'm a bit packed for today. How about Monday?"* (I was just covering up as I need to brush up on C language skills.)

Chitra replied, *"Oh thanks, Kaushik."* (Since Chitra joined, I started supporting Chennai Super Kings and my laptop password was changed to *'Chitra@123'*. Such was my love.)

We both parted ways with me seeing a partner in her, and she, a teacher in me. That's fine because your partner is your teacher too.

I came back to reality and remembered that both the task and the activity of cursing my boss were incomplete. So, I started working on the task and in parallel continued cursing my boss for 35 minutes for not onboarding Chitra onto the project much earlier.

09:00 PM, Same Day, and Workplace: After completing the final task, I rushed to the library and picked up the book titled, **"Basics of C Language"**. I was only left with 5 minutes for the last office shuttle. Without panicking, I walked calmly and was successful to catch the shuttle. (*This is what experience can do to you*)

09:50 PM, Same Day, and Home: I reached home and *Ananth* was busy taking a nap. I went to my room without making much noise. After his long lazy nap, he woke up, confirmed it was me and not a thief, and went back to take another nap. Ignoring him, I continued preparing from the book I bought from the library and it only took me 10 pages to realize that I don't have to brush up on my skills but I have to study from scratch.

After a few hours, *Ananth* woke up and came to my room. He saw me and was surprised by what I was doing as he never saw me studying because I never did. As they say, life comes in a full circle. It felt like a Déjà-vu with role reversal. A day earlier I was surprised to see Ananth's actions and he had a girl to meet, and today, he felt the same with my actions and I have a girl to meet. ***"Woah, when did you start studying or are you acting?"*** unlike me, *Ananth* didn't hold it back, he said it to my face.

I spent the entire weekend preparing technical skills to impress and soft skills to express. For the first time, I felt the weekend to be passing slowly. A wise man whom I see in the mirror said, ***'Time passes like a Porsche when you want it to slow down, and like a bullock cart when you want it to move fast.'***

09:21 PM, 10ᵗʰ Dec 2017, Sunday, Bedroom: All the preparation was done and I picked up my phone, scheduled the alarm for 06:20 AM for the next day, and changed the ringtone to *'Kaho Na Pyaar Ho'*.

06:20 AM, 11ᵗʰ Dec 2017, Monday, Bedroom, the D-Day, *Alarm rings*: Within a few seconds of the alarm, I was awake and within a few minutes of the day, I was ready and within a few hours, I was at the office.

09:21 AM, Same Day, and Workplace: I was the second one to the office and I saw Chitra at her desk, happier than her usual self. I walked up to her and we both exchanged greetings.

With no delay, she said, *"Bhaiyya, Good morning! How was your weekend, and what did you do? Looks like you are a bit late than usual. Btw, Hiranya helped me out with C Language basics; he's such a sweet guy."*

She spoke without a pause for 10 seconds with 5-6 questions in it, but all I could grasp was the word 'Bhaiyya.' I somehow still couldn't believe what she said and I felt I heard it wrong. But there's no one else on the floor. I stayed silent and she was confused about why I stayed silent.

Seeing me silent, she asked, *"Bhaiyya, Bhaiyya what happened? Are you alright?"*

I couldn't take it anymore. The number of times she called me **"Bhaiyya"** kept increasing. With genuine courage and a not-so-genuine smile, I responded, *"Ah! Nothing, who's Hiranya?"*

She replied, *"Oh! He too was joining our project, and ironically, he's from Chennai too. I met him in the corridor while I was conversing with my parents on phone, and he approached me. We are now the best of buddies and luckily, he knows C Language and helped me with all the training and queries too."* I had three questions for myself.

The first question was, *'I wondered how many people my boss was on boarding. Are we by any chance building a satellite?'*

The second question was, *'Why don't such coincidences happen in my life? Never did a girl approach me when I was conversing in English.'*

Before I had the last question and the first teardrop, I replied, *"Oh! Okay, good luck. See you then."* For the first time, I wished my boss gave me more work to help me deviate from the thoughts of Chitra.

A month later, Chitra came up to my desk and told *"Bhaiyya! Hiranya and I are in a relationship. I felt like sharing with you."* I didn't know how to react and not look awkward; I congratulated her and continued focusing on my work.

11:21 AM, 19ᵗʰ Jan 2018, Friday, Mumbai, Workplace: Yet another week with the same routine. And, again, I felt someone tapping on my shoulder. I thought to myself, *"If it's Chitra, the only word she'd get to hear is I'm busy."* But it was Keerthi from Kolkata, another beautiful girl on the floor. Wondering how I know her? (Just after the heartbreak episode of Chitra, I replaced my office crush with Keerthi who's from Kolkata. I changed my laptop password to *'Keerthi@123'* and my favorite IPL team was Kolkata Knight Riders.)

And, Keerthi repeated the same thing as Chitra. She too joined our project recently, and my boss recommended me for the training and she has some queries in C ++ language. Seeing the number of people being onboarded, I was sure we are not building any satellites but we are building a nuclear missile and my boss was hiding it from me. Anyway, I replied, *"Hey Sure, I will help you out. I'm a bit packed for today.*

How about Monday?" (Same reason again. I had to study to help her). She agreed to it with a smile and I reciprocated the same. We both parted ways, and the first thing I did was to enquire if there was a guy who could speak Bengali on our floor. Fortunately, there wasn't one.

I am a man who follows a routine. Hence, I ran to the library, picked up the book I needed, and started preparing for the big day again.

The only change was I didn't pick up the book **'Basics of C++'** but I picked up the book **'*Learn basics of Bengali'*.**

Moral of the Story: *Local Language is more powerful than Computer Language.*

4

Gratitude

07:45 AM, 11ᵗʰ Jun 2018, Monday, Delhi, Hostel, in the middle of a war: Yeah, you read it right. I was in the middle of a war. I was fighting a mental battle between lying back in bed and going to class. I had a class at 8:15 AM, my attendance was 50% and the temperature outside was 3 degrees. I had to choose between attending the class and continue lying on the bed. After a group discussion with my two personalities ('The obedient student who wanted me to go to class' vs. 'The lazy guy who wanted me to get some sleep'), I got up from the bed, walked a few steps with all the motivation, switched off the fan and jumped back on the bed. I decided to get more sleep. Not sure, where will my second personality take me in life.

The first thing I did while lying on the bed was to drop a message in the hostel Whatsapp group, ***"Let's skip the first hour and have breakfast! 'Health is wealth'."*** 40% of them said yes (They were just waiting for someone to initiate to avoid the guilt), and the rest didn't respond (They were still sleeping. Forget about the first hour, they'd come only post lunch).

For the first time in the semester, we went to the mess and had breakfast. We tried everything out there and reached on time for the second lecture. The professor, who was already in the class, asked us about the assignment. We had no clue we had an assignment. We replied saying, ***"We forgot sir. Sorry!"*** He replied, ***"Did you guys forget to have breakfast?"*** Oh no, the only time we ever had breakfast was today and we were asked this question. Professor kicked us out of the class. I stayed back in the corridor as my attendance for his course was even lower at 40% and I had to convince him to attend.

I tried paying attention to the lecture from outside, and the topic was, 'Gratitude.' Professor was stressing about how important it is for us to thank moments we cherished in life. It made me think through the past and reminisce about moments which I cherished. I also thought why not share a few moments which we all would have cherished at some stage in life?

1. Schooling: I guess one place where we made some great memories without even realizing it. Coming 1st in the class (Never did I get through), sitting only beside your buddy, debating over the favorite cartoon character, not having to wear a uniform on birthdays, awkward moments like standing on the bench in front of the entire class, waiting for that one sports period of the week, getting to accompany your friend for distributing birthday chocolates, forging parents' signature on the progress cards and planning summer holidays. #SchoolIsCool

2. Sports: Take a pause and look at your knees. You'll have at least one scar which dates back to the times

when you got hurt while playing your favourite sport. Remember the moment? Diving for your team to save a run or jumped awkwardly to score a goal for your team, or from any other sporting moment of yours. They don't give you pain anymore, but they carry some priceless moments from the past. Those were the moments where you gave all-in for the sport, for the team, for the win and yourself. You can't get those days back. Now when you look back, you'd be glad to have put in all that effort. Sometimes, scars make you smile too! We all have scars. Good or bad, on the skin or the heart, they all are great memory. Few helped you with victory, and few with a lesson. #CareYourScars

3. First Love: Recollect your first crush. Irrespective of where you ended up with your first love, it is a magical moment. All that planning to just say "Hi" to her/him, figuring out ways to impress them, the first conversations, the exchange of messages/ calls, the low budget but high valued dates and the long walks. For sure, those were the best moments then. Now when you look back, it brings a smile to you because first love is always magical. #PehlaPehlaPyaar

4. First Job: Life moves so fast and with a blink of an eye, we would move from schooling to job. Can you think of the moment, when you are done with the interview process and were eagerly waiting for the result? And, finally, the list comes out and you see your name. It would be a lie if you tell me that

you didn't cry. You might switch multiple times in your career, but there is no feeling like the first job. Right?

5. Strangers: More often than not, we miss out on thanking strangers around us. It just slips away. But, there's a lot of contribution from strangers who aren't your family/friends for you to be where you are now. Remember your aunt/uncle from the neighbourhood who cooked delicious food for you, all those professors who kept you pushing in academics, all the great chefs who satisfied your taste buds, the doctor who brought you down to earth without whom you would never be able to see the face of the earth. Family and friends make your life lovable, but kind strangers make your life livable.

You don't go to school again. You might never play your favourite sport again. Live your life, as you might never get a chance to relive it again. Be thankful for whatever you had in life, and whatever you cherished in life.

I realized I went on a trip of nostalgia and reminisced about moments and people of the past and it looks like the lecture is over and I felt like thanking the professor for kicking me out. Else, I wouldn't have thought about gratitude and I wouldn't be thanking the people and moments I cherished. Hence, I walked up to the professor and thanked him. He was confused about why I was behaving weirdly.

Moral of the Story: *Don't take gratitude for granted.*

5

Hostel, Thoda Pyaar Thoda Magic!

11:30 AM, 10th May 2019, Friday, Hyderabad Railway Station: I just completed my post-graduation and took the train back home. Like always, my father came to the station to receive me. And it was evident how proud he was about my post-graduation. Little did he know about my grades. I was a 6-pointer, and just to sound good I told my mom that I am a 7-pointer. And she told all my relatives about me being an 8-pointer and to the parents of possible alliances as a 9-pointer. All it took was a pinch of my mother's love to increase my CGPA from 6 to 9.

12:30 PM, Same day, Home: We reached home and my mom gave me a reception just like Jaya Bachchan from Kabhi Khushi Kabhi Gham. Unlike the movie, my father didn't ask me to take up the family business. As we didn't have a business of our own and even if we had one, he would have been very sure to not hand it over to me knowing my skills.

05:30 PM, Same day, Terrace, Enjoying Sunset: At college, you pick up many habits; one of them which I picked was smoking. And I smoked one every evening around sunset. Hence is why I enjoy sunsets. I locked the terrace door, lighted the cigar, and started smoking. In the meanwhile, on the terrace of the next building, I saw Shruthi and waved to her with a big smile and a half-burnt cigar. She responded back with a big smile but without a cigarette. She was busy on her mobile and I was busy with my cigarette. She was polluting sound and I was polluting the air. I focused on my cigarette and she, on her call

07:20 PM, Same Day, Reading Newspaper, and Home: I was going through the sports section while my father watched it from a distance and felt very proud. Phew! It's easy to make my father feel proud. Little did he know what I was reading. *'Does Rohit Sharma hate Virat Kohli?'* was the article I was reading and my mother from the other room shouted, *'Ravi! Come to the living room'*. I heard it but did not respond as I was in the middle of reading something important. And, my mom then screamed, *'Ravi! Come here. Shruthi came for you.'* I dropped the newspaper, left Rohit Sharma, Virat Kohli, and the article, and ran to the living room. I was scared about Shruthi complaining about my smoking.

Without wasting a second, I turned towards her and asked, *'What's up? Tell me how I can help you?'* She responded by saying, *'I got a seat in the same college as yours. But I never lived outside of the home and I'm very scared to live in a hostel. I am a little nervous and I came to you for some guidance on the same.'*

When a girl comes up to me and asks for guidance, I'd never say no even if she's asking about rocket science.

I wanted to be honest with her. But If I talk about all that in my house, my proud father will kick me out. Hence,

I asked her out for a walk to which she agreed. We both headed out and I started talking about Hostel life. She was anxious and I was energized.

"Hostel life is like India vs. Pakistan cricket match. It's beautiful, memorable and gives you moments to live for. Hostels can change the personality of a person in two months which his/her parents couldn't change in two decades. Sounds like a bigger transformation than HULK, right?"

"First few days of your hostel life are the most organized. You'll be new, alone and you will have an organized schedule. Something like waking up early in the morning, having breakfast, attending college, giving a ring to your parents post-college, studying, and having 8 hours of sleep. But then, by the end of the semester, you'd have made some wonderful friends and your schedule gets messed up. You'll have breakfast during lunchtime, study for only 15 minutes that too before the exam, ring your parents only during festivals, and attend college once in blue moon. But then, you will fall in love with this schedule, only because you'll have a bunch of friends around you who'll make your life easy and happy."

"Hostel life will make you understand the importance of resources. For the first month, you'll keep your bucket, mug, toothpaste, slippers, problems, worries, and grief to yourself. But post that, everything is everyones. There's nothing called personal. You'll make friends who'll take both your toothpaste and worries and treat them as their own. What better can you ask for?"

"Birthdays would be extremely exciting; you'll have 30-40 people waiting to beat you blue and black. And that is how they express love. You'll be asked to cut a cake worth 30 rupees. But, trust me; you'll never forget that day. Not because of the 30-rupee cake, but because of the effort put in by the 30 people. Your friend's mom will send an additional pack of sweets for you post-vacation. Your friend's father will check on your well-being while he checks on his kid. You will find a family in your friend's family."

"At times, you'll dislike the hostel food but eating together will make you love it. You'll have many 5-star hotel breakfasts post your college, but none will match your hostel breakfast."

"Your room/floor will become a cricket stadium, bar, study room, theatre, and whatnot depending upon the need of the hour. I remember 8 of us binge-watching Game of Thrones with vodka beside us just a night before our internals. Fast forward to today, I don't remember Game of thrones or the internal exams, all I remember are the memories I made on that day."

"There'll be times when the entire floor plays devotional songs just before the exams while playing Sheila ki Jawaani just after the exam. You'd see utmost attention from the entire hostel on both times."

"A 6 by 6 hostel room will give you memories worth till you get into your 6 feet grave. Life teaches how to grow, and Hostel life teaches you how to grow together. You'll miss home when you're leaving for the hostel for the first time,

and you'll miss the hostel when you're leaving for the last time."

And, with this, we completed a walk of 4 miles, and I completed sharing my experience from my 4 years of the hostel. Shruthi was excited about what I shared. She thanked me and we both walked back to our home. Shruthi ran to her house all excited, and I walked onto the terrace for a cigarette.

Moral of the Story: Smoking is injurious to health and Hostel life is beneficiary for your health.

6

Pyaar Deewana Hota Hain!

02:30 PM, 13th Feb 2020, Thursday, Bengaluru: One of those days where it wasn't hectic. Btw, I work for an MNC in a team of 7. I realized Valentine's Day (14th Feb) is not the most important day for a couple but it is the previous day (13th Feb) because of all the planning that goes in. And, our team wasn't any different as all of us were busy planning. The only difference was my team members were planning for Valentine's Day, and as I was single, I was planning what to order for lunch. I opened the food ordering app and it notifies me, ***'Hey don't worry if you didn't find Love, you can find Biryani for sure. Use coupon SingleForever for 200 rupees off.'*** I was so *angry* with the food ordering app for making fun of me and decided to never use the app. After 10 minutes, I felt *hungry* and used the coupon code 'SingleForever', to order Biryani worth 250 INR only for 50 INR. Anger and Hunger will make you do weird things. After 30 minutes, the delivery guy calls me and sounded half disappointed. And, while handing over the parcel, he looked to be completely disappointed. I asked him if he was expecting a girl. The poor guy replied 'No' and left. I had my Biryani and continued with the work. Meanwhile, everyone in the team applied for leave for the next day, and as I already disappointed the delivery guy, I didn't want to disappoint my team as well. Hence, I too applied for a leave. As time progressed, people left and the number of people in the corridor reduced drastically.

07:30 PM, Same Day, Workplace, 3 people at work: Phew, I wasn't the only one to be left working. If you see someone working on 13th February post 7 PM, they're either single or their boss has given them a lot of work. I winded up the work and left home.

07:45 PM, Same Day, Home: Wondering how I reached home so fast that too in Bengaluru? We took a flat for rent just 500 meters away from our workplace. That's the only way to skip traffic in Bengaluru. While I was entering the flat, I heard, *'Ishq wala Love'* song and few steps into the flat, I saw Marzook singing. He's a close friend of mine from college and he doesn't know Hindi at all (All that he knows is **Bhayya, Thoda Pyaaz Daalo**). I thought to myself, *"For sure, he has something planned for the 14th of Feb"*. I asked him, *"What Macha! What's the scene?"* He replied, *"Nothing Macha! This song is very soothing. I cooked for you and washed the utensils as well. You go and get freshen up."* The last time he was so sweet to me was on the first day of college when everyone acts very formally. If he's being so nice and sweet to me, a request or a favor is coming up soon. While I was thinking about what his plans are, he kept on being nice to me. With the amount of love he's showering on me; I wouldn't be surprised if he asks for my kidney.

I told him, *"See, if you are after my Liver or Kidney, with the amount of alcohol we drink, they're already damaged."*

He replied, *"No, No. I booked a movie ticket for you for tomorrow. I wanted you to enjoy yourself, and I didn't want to disturb you."* I asked him what he would do by sending me out. He replied, *"Yeah, Right! I would be alone. What should I do? I'll call my girlfriend over."*

Can anyone be more dramatic? I disagreed with his offer. After an argument of 10 minutes, I was forced to agree. I went to my room with the ticket, and he went to his with a smile.

08:30 PM, Same day, Bedroom: With not much work for the day, I opened YouTube and started watching '*Kal ho Na Ho*' for the 17th time in my life. Every time I watched it; I get awestruck by the unconditional love showered by SRK. YouTube was concerned about my eyes as it kept pausing the movie once every 15 minutes by running non-skippable ads. I closed my eyes while it played the non-skippable ads. All those ads were on flowers, cakes, bouquets and greeting cards. I was like, *'Who are you trying to sell to?'* The ads for the first time were boring, but the movie for the 17th time wasn't boring at all. SRK can do magic. The way SRK told *'Love yourself first before loving anyone else hit me hard'*. I went into a spiral of thoughts on the same before I dozed off.

11:17 AM, 14th Feb 2020, Friday, Bedroom: I woke up only on the 5th alarm. By my standards of waking up on an off day, I did pretty well. With half-open eyes, I noticed Marzook in the other room getting ready as he was paying a visit to SRK's house. I was like, *"Dude, I am the one to go out! Not you."*

He saw me being in shorts and I could sense him being anxious. I comforted him saying, **"Don't worry, I'd be out in 30."** He acknowledged with a wide smile and all his anxiety vanished. Phew, felt like a doctor who could treat anxiety.

11:27 AM, Same day, Bedroom: I got ready in a jiffy and I still had 20 minutes for the cut-off before Marzook threw me out. I looked at the clock and imagined how many people would be expressing their love at this very moment and here I am, in the hangover of '**Kal ho Na Ho**' from the previous night. And, after a 5-minute group discussion with SRK (imaginary), I decided to write a letter and express my love towards Priya.

I ran to the other room, and after 5 minutes, I found a piece of white paper and a pen. I thought for a few minutes and started capturing my love for Priya.

'To Priya,

I never expressed my love towards you but just don't think I don't love you. If there's anyone in this world I can love forever, it is you. And, you are the first person I turn out to in happiness and sorrow.

No one has handled me better than you. You always showered unconditional love and have been there for me whenever I hit rock bottom.

For cheering in my lows, for clapping in my highs, for trusting me when I'm in self-doubt and for calming me down when I'm in a rage.

I love you, and I will till the grave. You are the happiest when I'm kind to myself or trying to be happy or taking good care of myself. I know you'll feel complete if I take care of myself.

Thanks, Priya!

Yours Darshan'

11:35 AM, Same day, Bedroom: I was sure that Priya would love it. All I had to do now is to express what was written to Priya. I stood up, took a few steps, walked towards the mirror and started reading out the letter line-by-line. Priya listened carefully and by the end of it, I was happy and so was Priya.

Oh! Don't get confused, my name is **Priyadarshan**. It was a letter written by me to myself expressing how much I should love myself. Read the letter again, it will make more sense. It took me 29 years, 17 times of Kal ho Na Ho on the go, a Valentine's day and the lines of SRK **'Khud ko Pyaar Karo'** *to* realize how much I should love myself.

Priya in the mirror smiled and Darshan on the other side of the mirror smiled equally, not more; not less.

It's not only with me but with everyone. Every day, we should love and thank ourselves a little more. Because, only then, we'll be able to love others.

11:45 AM, Same Day, *staring at the mirror*: While I was enjoying the moment all by myself, I noticed a reflection of an angry face in the mirror. It was none other than Marzook. I then looked at the clock and realized it was time for me to run out of the house. I ran towards him and hugged him. He looked disappointed too, as he thought his first hug for the day would be from his girlfriend.

P. S: Whenever you try writing such letters, please ensure to write how this letter is for yourself. A friend of mine got too inspired and wrote the letter but forgot to mention his name. It basically was a love letter with no name. He thought if I am giving it to myself, why would I need the name? He wrote the letter, read it aloud, thanked himself and kept the letter in the cupboard. Everything went as per the plan. But, a few days later, his father found it. And, you know what happens a father gets hold of a love letter. Please ensure to hide such letters in a secret place.

P.S.S: Signing off, PriyaDarshan. People call me Darshan, and due to a glitch made by my 10th class teacher, I have my name on all the government ID cards as Priya D and I continued that everywhere (Even in food ordering apps). Now you know why the delivery guy was disappointed seeing me. Poor guy expected Priya!

7

The Real Life Horror

08:17 PM, 20th May 2022, Tiresome Friday, Hyderabad: I don't generally work hard on Fridays but this was an exception. I was breaking my head on the laptop for 30 minutes now. Oh! This isn't any professional work. This is all for my cousin's wedding as she was getting married in a couple of days.

Like most marriages in our country, the cousins of the bride/groom are the most hardworking people. And I am one such cousin for my cousin. And my uncle thought I was the smartest of all the cousins and handed me 3 lakhs INR and the responsibility of managing the needs during the event. Little did he know that I can't even manage my own finances and he's expecting me to manage such a huge amount? And hence is why I was banging my head to capture all the transactions from the last few days on a laptop in the wedding hall. I never used my laptop at the work properly and here I am using it in a wedding hall. And, after 30 minutes, I can account for the spending of only 2.6 lakh, and I have no account for the remaining 40 thousand. This doesn't seem right.

I re-checked everything and worked on it again. And, this time, I see a spending of 3.4 Lakh. This is even worse.

My uncle will for sure change his expectations of me seeing the calculations. I remembered a quote I tweaked, '**With great expectations come great responsibilities.**'

In the last 2 days, I only had 2 hours of sleep, but it was on a king-size bed though. The only problem was, there were 5 of my cousins already sleeping on it. So, I had very less space for myself on the bed. If I took a deep breath, I'd fall on a cousin who already fell on the floor because of his heavy breathing. So, to cover up for all the lost sleep, I was trying to take a nap in the wedding hall with my feet on the empty chairs.

It was a matter of seconds before I fell asleep. And, all of a sudden, I see some random uncle standing before me and uttering something. I thought it was a dream but then why will I have some random uncles come up in my dreams; instead, I'll have Kiara Advani come in my dreams. So, it was not my dream for sure. With great difficulty, I looked up and tried focusing on what he was saying and I heard, **"Hey! The chairs are not properly arranged, this is not how it should be done. You have to re-arrange them and I will guide you."**I wondered if I was hearing it wrong as I was half-asleep but then he had a disappointed expression as well. He had the confidence of being the third most important person in the wedding after the bride and groom. I thought of picking up a fight but then I don't know who he is and he looked capable to mess things around in the marriage. I decided not to pick up a fight instead I put up a smile and agreed on what he wanted.

And, after re-arranging all the 497 chairs as per his vision, he was satisfied, I was relieved and tired. Arranging chairs so many times made me feel like the owner of them and I choose two corner chairs, turned them to my convenience, kept my tired legs on them again and started preparing for a nap. Before I could fall asleep, all my cousins came over as their share of work was over. Most of them had good sleep as they had a good share on the King Size bed as well. Within two minutes, all I saw were 10 cousins, 20 legs and 20 chairs de-arranged with legs on them. Seeing chairs not being in order broke my heart. After all, the person who arranged 497 chairs twice knows the pain.

And, in a few seconds comes Priyanka, the cousin of the groom and insists everyone on having fun. And, I was ready for it. For a 29-year-old, who's been working tirelessly for days, the only thing he can remember when someone says 'Fun' is falling asleep. But then she wants to go to *'Bhool Bhullaya 2'* with all of us. Everyone out there nodded their heads in agreement and I nodded the other way in disagreement and no one cared though. My kind of fun was to hit the bed and see Kiara in my dreams and her kind of fun was to watch Kiara on the big screen.

I was always scared to watch horror movies but I was very courageous to skip them without any hesitation. In a few minutes, they decided on the theatre and time. I was running out of time and tried to bring in my negotiation skills. Let me tell you, I was very bad at negotiation skills. The highest I ever negotiated was 7 rupees, only because the price of the product was 207 and the shopkeeper didn't have sufficient change. But I felt this to be the right moment. Else, I will be pulled over to a horror movie half-asleep and by the end of it, I'd be half-dead too with fear.

And, after 10 minutes of extensive negotiation from my end, the group disagreed. And, as a last resort, I blackmailed them by saying to stay back as I'm scared and they can go if they wish to leave out their brother. It didn't take much time for them to change their decision. No, they didn't drop the plan of going to a horror movie; they dropped the plan of taking me along. I was happy with their decision. I now have all of the king-size bed for myself (at least for 3 hours). One of the cousins asked me if I was going out with a girl. I replied dramatically saying, ***"My cousins are my family. I will be missing you guys"***. I even faked tears for intensity and half of them were convinced.

And, in fifteen minutes, all of them left leaving those unorganized chairs as-is. I rearranged those chairs and before the uncle sees them again, I ran to the bedroom like Usain Bolt and jumped into it. Nothing in the world can wake me up now. The ticking sound of the clock was in sync with my dozing eyes. And, in those few seconds, I switched on the Wi-Fi and opened Whatsapp; most of the messages didn't excite me except for one. The one from *Havya*, who was my colleague at work and lives in the same city. (We are almost into a relationship). My eyes lit up seeing her message and all my sleep vanished. She said, ***"Hey Anurag, How about watching a movie?"***

"Woah, even I was about to ask you for a movie as I was bored too", was my reply from the bed with eyes half-closed. Like a wise man who arranged all those chairs twice once said, **"Love makes you do crazy things."**

She knew me being at my cousin's wedding and she asked, ***"Will any of your cousins accompany us?"*** Even if they want to, why would I want them to? I replied, ***"No, no, they're scared to come for a late-night show. Kids these days are a bit scared for everything."*** She replied, ***"Oh, glad you're courageous at least. I'll go ahead and book the tickets then. Be ready in 20 minutes, I'll pick you up."*** I felt a little guilty for defaming my cousins, and hence I dropped a message in the cousin's Whatsapp group, ***"Missing you guys."*** I jumped out of the bed, got ready and waited for her. And, in 20 minutes, she was at my place, and we both left for the theatre. I didn't even care to ask her which movie it was. It didn't seem important to me.

We reached on time, found our seats, and settled in. And, in 5 minutes, ads started coming up and then came the national anthem. Only then did I realize that the national anthem will be played before the movie. I never knew it as I was always late to the movies. Whenever I went to the movies, by the time I reached; it would have been either the introduction song or the fight. **'Pros of having a girlfriend who's punctual'**

And, then the title card came and it was **'Bhool Bhullaya 2'**. Out of all, she had to book this. I looked at her face in fear and she was all excited. **'Cons of having a girlfriend who loves horror movies'**

I didn't watch the screen even for a second. All I did was look at Havya. By the end of the first song, she asked me what was wrong. I replied, **"Why will I watch the movie when you are beside me?"** She thought I'm flirting but it was one of the two reasons. Fear of not being able to watch a horror movie is the other one. Havya watched Karthik Aryan and Kiara Advani on screen and I watched my own Kiara Advani in Havya. The first half passed in a jiffy and it was the interval.

Both of us, hand-in-hand, walked to the canteen to buy some popcorn. And, I felt someone tapping on my shoulder. I turned around with a smile and then I saw my cousins with popcorn in their hands and anger on their faces. If it wasn't theatre, and if it wasn't my cousin's wedding in two days, it would've been my death day for sure. And, to add it up, Havya holds my hand firmly. This was more of a shocker to my cousins. She didn't know they are my cousins and she said, ***"How different are you from your cousins! They are scared to watch a late-night show movie and you are watching a horror movie on a late-night show."***

Before she spoke, I was a little hopeful of surviving, but now. I lost all hope. For the first time, I wanted her to not talk. I somehow calmed her and with all my sign language skills which she couldn't grasp. I begged my cousins to stay silent with the same sign language and they obliged. I didn't know what was scarier, the remaining part of the movie or the remaining part of my life post-the movie.

And, for the entire second half, I didn't watch Havya but I watched the movie. The horror scenes in the movies didn't make me feel scared anymore. I was more scared about what would happen when I reach home. By the end, all I hoped was for my cousins to not get inspired by how

Tabu was dragged and beaten and all I prayed was for them to not use the chairs to hit me. If I passed out, who'll re-arrange the chairs? Within no time, the reel life in the movie ended, and my real-life started.

Moral of the Story: They say, *"Love takes you to places."* Be careful where it takes you to.

Advice: It's always better to ask the name of the movie well in advance.

8

Software Engineer. The Person You Know, the Journey You Don't

08:45 PM, 18th Dec 2022, Sunday, Hyderabad, Balcony: To have to work on a Sunday is the worst feeling ever. But then your boss saying, ***"Let's call it a day"*** after a stressful day is an equally good feeling.

I shut my laptop as hard as I can and walked towards the balcony to have a glimpse of the city I live on the 17th floor and it looks pretty up there. My taste is good in such things. I mean, my landlord's taste is good in buying such apartments.

By the way, the reason my boss called it off a day was that he wanted to watch the FIFA world cup final between Argentina and France. And, I have very little football knowledge. If you rank me against a newborn baby on football skills, both of us would stand equal. I only knew 4 football players, Christiano Ronaldo, Lionel Messi, Sunil Chhetri and my friend Sajil Sathyanathan. Ignoring all this, I enjoyed the silence amid chaos from the balcony.

09:30 PM, Same day, *someone ringing the bell continuously*: Whosoever it might be, they're dead in my hands today (*except for my landlord*). I ran from the balcony to the main door like Messi and opened the door. I raised my hand to catch hold of the person by the collar and just as I opened the door, I saw my boss. Instead of lowering my hand, I raised another hand, hugged him, and welcomed him. He owns a flat in the same apartments but on the 7th floor. It feels great to be better/higher than your boss at least in a few things. My boss knows about me having a very big TV set at my place. He wanted to watch the match along with our teammates on my big screen. He took an effort of inviting all of our team and within a few minutes, everyone arrived and started watching football.

10:00 PM, Same day, Living Room: With every passing minute of the game, there was tension building in the room and I too was tense, but not about the match. I was a bit nervous about the next day as it was an important day for me. Post the match, everyone thanked my boss and left. Shouldn't they be thanking me? Anyway, I thought my boss would thank me at least. Instead, he thanked himself for organizing such an event. No wonder!

All of them loved Messi and I hated the mess they created in my flat. Ignoring all of it, I jumped on to the bed leaving the mess as-is and within minutes I fell asleep.

07:17 AM, 19th Dec 2022, Monday, Bedroom: Woke up 43 minutes earlier than usual. As I told you, it was an important day for me. I was supposed to meet a girl to try and impress her. My dad had some connections and he set this meeting up for me. This was all for my better future. As I was getting ready, I felt a little stressed. To calm myself I texted my dad, ***"Love you."*** He responded with a Thumbs up emoji. Huh! *'A typical dad reaction.'* Now, I was completely stressed. I tried another way; I opened YouTube and looked up some videos on meditation.

Meditation looked very tough. I barely watched for 5 minutes and lost patience. I realized that I first need to meditate to develop the patience to watch meditation videos online. Anyway, I groomed myself the best and reached my destination. After 10 minutes of waiting, I met and greeted her with all my heart, and she did the same. She was very curious to know about my professional experience, personal journey, interests and hobbies. After 30 minutes and 40 questions (I had 4 and she had 36) the conversation ended. She told me she'll get back to me and I left back to my current workplace.

Sounds romantic right? Take a pause; if you were thinking about me meeting a prospective match, you were wrong. I was talking about an interview with an HR which my dad got it scheduled through his connections. Read the previous paragraph with this context now. It will make much more sense.

10:01 AM, Same day, Workplace: I reached my current workplace and was feeling a little doubtful about my performance. I entered the lift, pressed the 10th floor, and started retrospection. By the time I reached the 3rd floor, I thought, ***"If I am a little lucky, I should get the job."*** By the time, I reached the 6th floor, I thought, ***"I did pretty well at the interview and I for sure should get the job."*** And, by the time I reached the 10th floor, I thought, ***"I killed the interview and it's their loss if they miss out on giving me an***

offer." It took me only 10 floors and 10 seconds to become over-confident from under-confident.

I entered the cubicle and all my colleagues acted a little surprised to see me so nicely groomed. The reason being, I came so professionally only twice ever. One, on the day of joining, and two, when my boss informed us about a new girl joining our team.

A couple of hours into the day, I noticed an email with the subject, **'Share your experience from Software Industry'**. I was so confident about the interview from the morning and I thought, **"I will however resign, so it wouldn't matter if I'm a little honest about it."** I wanted to go all in and capture all of them. And, I started typing them.

Here you go:

1. **<u>Strong Fundamentals:</u>** A major part of the first year in the IT industry is spent filling out excel sheets, adjusting font size in the deck, and creating documentation which will anyway be rejected by the leadership team. I'm sure the greatest of the greats would have done the same in their first few years in IT.

2. **<u>Roller Coaster Ride:</u>** Normal people take escalators to go up. Software engineers get escalations to make sure they don't go up the ladder. Normal people chase flights, trains, and opposite genders. We, software engineers, chase shuttles and cabs all the time.

3. **<u>Honeymoon Period:</u>** If a software engineer is carefree, there are only two reasons. She/he must have been in the notice period or is still in the initial onboarding phase. The onboarding period is like; you'll be scared if you'd make a mistake, whereas the Notice period is about not being scared even if you make a mistake. Don't go and make a mistake now!

4. **<u>Stay Calm and Trust Luck:</u>** Only 10% of the software engineers get to go abroad and the rest 90% support the onsite team in onshore time zones. Its fine, if it's not written for you, it can't happen. But make sure you have good connections with your onshore friends. Force them to get chocolates for you while they visit you. Always go for Ferrero Rocher. I've been getting them for 5 years now.

5. **<u>Don't miss Cultural days:</u>** Doesn't matter if you don't come to the office on a client visit but make sure to go on the cultural days for sure. You'd get to see your office crush in traditional wear.

6. **<u>Be Quick:</u>** Finding some place in the canteen and getting a place in the elevator need some agility. So, be quick.

7. **<u>Customer is God:</u>** For obvious reasons, clients are no less than gods. Clients are only the third set of people I ever tried to impress in my life. The first one is the prospect father-in-law in arranged marriage setups, and the second one was the HR in the morning.

8. __Nothing lasts forever:__ Your salary and your weekend too are temporary. They both last only for a limited time. And, this happens all your life. Nothing lasts forever. So, get used to it. Also, leaves won't get approved forever. So, get creative and plan your sick leaves accordingly. Avoid reasons like fever and cough. 90% of us use it as a first resort.

9. __Maintain Good Rapport with HR:__ HR is the only person who'll come to your rescue when you are in trouble. So, make good friendships with HR. Just friendships, nothing more.

10. __Stay Hungry:__ Ah! Not what you think. Skip breakfast if you can on the team lunch days. You can eat more. I don't have dinner on the previous day to keep my stomach empty.

The Software Industry changed definitions of some Basic English words. Scrum, Agile, Bean, Class, Tester, Story, and Bug are very different to what I learnt in childhood. And, there are a few things we get without putting effort once we join the IT industry. Body Fat, Hair loss and Credit Card offerings.

And, with this, I took a pause and waited for the right moment to hit send. In the meanwhile, my boss informed me about a project kick-off meeting scheduled in 15 minutes. I laughed to myself and murmured, **"Absolutely not doing it"** as I was confident about the interview. Just then, I received a call from the HR who interviewed me in the morning and she, in a sweet voice said, ***"Hi, It was an absolute pleasure having a conversation with you.***

I really cherished the time and enjoyed it. And, looking at the current scenario, we deeply regret to inform you that we can't proceed with the next rounds. But we are looking forward to having you in future if any openings come up." I was confused if I should feel sad about the rejection or feel happy about the way she rejected me. This will go down as my sweetest rejection ever. I was feeling sad for my father though for all his efforts.

I was glad to have not hit the send button yet. With no delay, I deleted all the learnings and did 5 minutes of meditation. Phew, learning meditation didn't go to waste. I went into the meeting which my boss was looking forward to. And, all I told him about the next project was, **"Absolutely doing it."** That's how life is.

Please let me know in case of any concerns and have a nice day. Oops, I got used to it.

P.S: Cheers to everyone out there who's making progress to achieve dreams of self or of loved ones! Hope you enjoyed this piece and please don't take any of it to heart.

Thanks & Regards

A Software Engineer

9

Serial Killer (29, Male)

Yes, you read it right. This is a story of a serial killer. And, it is about me. I have been a serial killer for 15 years now. I've been waiting for a long time now to confess who I actually am. And what better platform than this book? Don't call the cops right away, just wait till the end.

My first attempt at killing dates back to the times when I was 16 and the last attempt was a few months back. All my attempts were successful except for the last one. Somehow, he lived. I'll even confess how this kid managed to stay alive (You'll get to know it by the end of the story).

Also, don't be scared. If you're reading this, you were never on my radar. And, like most serial killers I too have a few specifications about who I wanted to kill. It was always the kids and no one else. A fun fact, I am yet to be suspected and there was no evidence at all. A serious fact, no one but only the murderer and the murdered were aware of the killings. The murderer can't tell anyone, and the murderer never told anyone. No traces of fingerprints, foot marks, or blood stains; nothing whatsoever. One might find gold if they start digging but not the traces.

No one ever wants to be a serial killer. It's a profession by force and not by choice. The same was the case with me as well and when I attempted it for the first time, I was forced and wanted it to be the last time. But, once I started, none of the killings was the last one. And, trust me, society wasn't feeling bad either about what I did.

It all started when I was in 10th standard. And, like most kids of that age, I loved cricket more than anything else. But **Mr. Society** and his daughter **Ms. Fear** came into my life. They had no relevance in my life and they were not more than strangers. Good scores on the cricket ground brought me joy and happiness whereas good grades in my academics made both Mr. Society and Ms Fear happier. They kept asking me, ***"Don't you have the fear about your future?"*** I had my answer which was, ***"I'd manage somehow."*** But then, they brought in words like, 'Competition, Security and Risk.' And, I had no answer.

After an exhausting mental battle, I requested them to stay silent and stop bothering me. This was the moment they were waiting for and they replied, ***"We'll not bother you if you commit a murder."*** Sounded scary but seemed to be a fair deal for a 16-year-old kid. With a long deep breath, I took in some oxygen, thought for a few seconds, and left both carbon dioxide and cricket. I then shifted my focus to academics. I killed the kid in me who would've taken cricket seriously as a career. I got good grades, but all I had was only grades and no cricket.

Two years down the line, in 12th standard, I developed an interest in filmmaking. I almost made up my mind to pursue filmmaking seriously. And, again, Mr. Society and Ms. Fear were back with their son-in-law (**Mr. Failure**). I was amazed by their timing and all they had was similar questions with higher intensity. Must appreciate how disciplined and committed they were. They were asking question after question on uncertainties of my future by taking turns. And, all of them were about the uncertainties of my future. They were so concerned about my future and I didn't have answers this time as well. And, it was the same deal again, I commit murder and they'll not bug me with the questions for the time being. What else could I do? I again ended up killing the kid in me who wanted to pursue filmmaking. Guess what, no one except me knew it. Unfortunately, I was the one killing and I had to go through immense pain. Weird stuff, I know! I killed the kid inside just like how it's done in movies. No traces but only tears. No fingerprints but only memories. All three of them were happy and left me alone for a few years.

Years passed and they kept coming and I kept killing. Now, when I look back, all I have is memories of murders. I now have a decent job, with sufficient money, and support from family/friends but when I randomly stop at a traffic signal waiting for the signal to turn green, the 100 seconds of wait time takes me back by 10 years and keeps me reminding about what I lost in the process. (***Happiness and Satisfaction***)

Couple of months back, I fell in love with writing and wanted to spend time on it and I was sure all the family members of **Mr. Society** would come again. And before I even started writing, they were here again. And, like always, they almost convinced me to kill the kid in me who loved to write. I almost killed the kid and when the kid was about to take his last breath, a thing struck my mind and I replied, ***"But, I'll be happy and satisfied"***. All of them went numb and quiet with this single line, the kid jumped back to life, and I had peace. This was the kid I was referring at the start of the story who is still alive.

Moral of the Story: To the ones being bothered by society, Fear, Failure and Peer pressure. Remember it's okay to get low grades and earn little, but it is not okay to kill your passion. Irrespective of the stage of your life, there will be questions about the uncertainty of your future. There is a reason why we say 'Future is uncertain' because no one knows what happens in future. If no one knows what happens in future, why spoil the present? Your Present is the past of your future. Don't ruin it! Remember, you'll have to make the 7-and 70-year-old version of you proud. Don't kill the kid in you. Don't leave your hobbies and interests.

Yes, Life is a race. But the only race we all are in is to die. No one knows who's dying, how and when. And, you can't win the race against time. So, Life is a race but run at your own pace, pursue your passions, capture those little moments, stay happy, feel satisfied and someday die! End of the story!

P.S: Hope you don't call the cops now!

Signing Off,

Your Serial Killer

10

The Leave Love Letter

08:00 PM, 05th **Feb 2023, Sunday, Hyderabad, Living Room:** One of those Sundays where I wasn't worried about Monday. I work for an MNC and have a lot of deliverables for the next day but I was calm. It was not because I was ahead of the schedule but it was because I already planned for sick leave. And, by my side on the bed is my 10-year-old daughter **Kriti**. For her age, she has a lot of toys to keep her busy. But today, she wants to become an *'English Teaser'* (English Teacher it is). Hence, I am her student and she's my English teacher, I realized I am her toy today. And, she asked me to write a letter and give it to her mom and I obliged.

It's been more than two decades since I wrote a letter. The last time I wrote a letter was in Class 7 to *Meghana* to express my feelings for her. She was my classmate, and neighbor and I liked her very much.

Just to set the context, my English back then was terrible. The best I could communicate was 'Hit for four by Sachin, Happy Birthday, and All Indians are my brothers and (coughs) sisters.' But Meghana was very proficient with communication. I struggled to pass English while she taught the failures during free hours. Not a bad time to fail and sit in classes taught by the girl you like. Meghana was beautiful and talented.

***Don't know the time, date or month*, 7th Class, 4th Period:** I thought to give Meghana the letter I wrote during lunch break. But then, our progress reports were distributed in the same period and as usual, I failed in English. I looked at Meghana and saw her crying. And on seeing that, I dropped the idea of giving the letter.

The same day, 7th Class, Lunch Break: I went up to her and asked why she was crying. She showed me her progress report pointing at the C grade in Chemistry. I was very good at chemistry; I got a B grade. I was trying to console her. Such contrast lives, I failed in a subject and am consoling her while she got a C grade and was being consoled by me. She looked at my progress report and asked, *"Hey Vardhan. Can you please explain Chemistry?"* My brain couldn't comprehend any further than my name. Not because of my attraction towards her, but because of the speed she spoke. I nodded in agreement not knowing what she asked for.

And, she replied, *"See you at your place around 7 PM. Please teach me the basics."* I didn't want to be looked like a fool, so I paid attention to what she said and memorized the sentence. We both parted ways. I ran to Murali (a close friend of mine who I thought had better skills of communication than me. Usually, I get an F grade in English whereas Murali gets an E grade). I repeated the sentence Meghana told and asked Murali what she exactly meant. Murali replied, *"What did you do? She coming to home yours 7 PM to complain to your father"*. I and Murali spent the entire second half of the day analyzing why Meghana wanted to complain. And, when the final bell rang, we gave up on brainstorming, I thanked Murali for all the emotional support and went back home.

6:45 PM, Same evening, My bedroom: I was a little worried about my Father. Confused? So, for the day I already made sure my father had one headache which was to handle my progress report. He for sure will get stressed looking at it. And, in our home, we have an organized schedule whenever the progress reports are distributed. It's a 2-hour activity. First 30 minutes, I muster all the courage and show them, next 30 seconds, they are happy with the grades in all but English. Next 30 minutes, they scold me by warning me about my future. And, the final 1 hour, their love dominates their anger, and they pamper me. So, I was worried about how my father would handle both the complaint from Meghana and low grades in English simultaneously. I didn't want my dad to go through that. After all, I love my dad and I wanted him to be peaceful. I had to avoid one of the two things. Just for the sake of my father, I forged his signature on the progress report and waited for Meghana to come and complain.

7:00 PM, Same Night, Main Door, *Doorbell Rings*: I was sure it was Meghana. Hmm, Meghana wasn't only beautiful and talented but she was also punctual. My mother opened the door and welcomed her into the living room. I heard some whispers but didn't dare to hear them from close. In no time, my mother came up to me and I was curious to know what the complaint was all about. My mother in our native language said, ***"Did you tell Meghana that you'll explain Chemistry? She's here. Go help her with it. I will make some snacks for you both."*** My first reaction wasn't excitement but anger. I was furious with Murali as I realized how I unnecessarily gave him VIP status thinking he had better skills of communication. He was only as good as me and he didn't have better skills than me; all he had was better luck than me to get an E grade. In no more than 10 seconds, I shifted my focus to Meghana and rushed to the living room with a small jump and a big smile.

8:00 PM, Same Night, Living Room: I explained to her all that I know in the language that I know (Telugu). Told her, it'll be easy if I explain it in Telugu (the Native Language for both of us). After 45 minutes of explanation of Chemistry and 15 minutes of discussion on Shaktiman (It was her favorite show) we decided to call it a day. And, she left the place.

Luckily for me, the chemistry syllabus was so huge, it required frequent sessions. With every session, both, her love for Chemistry and my love for her grew. On one lazy Sunday, I was watching Shaktiman and got motivated. And, I thought, come what may, I will express my thoughts to Meghana the next time we meet.

10:00 AM, The next day, 7th Class, and Lunch Break: I walked up to her and told her, ***"Meghana, I know no English. I only know broken English."*** Meghana replied, ***"So what? All of us are good in a lot and bad in a few. I will teach you English. Don't worry."*** I realized; Meghana wasn't only Beautiful, Talented, and Punctual but was also Kind. Oh!

If you were thinking I'd tell her about my feelings for her, you're wrong. I needed to watch Shaktiman thrice to muster the courage to tell her. We then tweaked our sessions a little. It was 45 minutes of Chemistry, 15 minutes of Shaktiman and 45 minutes of English. Things went well, Shaktiman kept saving the world, and Meghana kept becoming my world.

Years later, our paths changed, I pursued engineering, and she pursued literature. I never expressed my feelings for her nor did I give the letter I wrote to her. Finally, one day, she got married. And, eventually, I too got married. That's how life is.

I even attached a picture of Meghana in her 20's which I liked the most. I never dared to give the letter to her and still have it secretly stored in my cupboard. The letter, the love, the picture and the moments were all with me.

09:20 PM, 05th **Feb 2023, Sunday, Hyderabad, Living Room, and Back to Present:** I had a tear in my eye remembering all that. But then, I realized I was running out of time given by my daughter's teacher. And, I didn't even start the letter. And in the background, I saw my daughter watching Shaktiman on my mobile. She assured me to give the phone back only if I complete the letter. I was in no mood to write one now. Instead, I thought I'll go give the love letter I wrote for Meghana to my wife. After all, a love letter is a love letter. (My wife knows about my childhood friend Meghana. But she doesn't know about the letter that I wrote. In fact, my wife knows more about Meghana than me.)

I walked towards the cupboard, picked the letter up, cleaned the dust and ran towards my wife. Before she realized, why I am being a little awkward, I handed her the letter. And, she started reading it. The entire letter only had one sentence and a picture. It made her laugh and cry at the same time.

My daughter saw this, threw the phone on the bed, left Shaktiman to himself, came up to us and took the letter into her hands and screamed, ***"Mumma, Dad wrote 'I Love you' and it has your name and your photo. Do you know Daddy before marriage?"***

I got married to the same Meghana from my childhood. I didn't dare to express my feelings but Meghana had the courage. Over that period, I developed my English skills all because of her, and she developed feelings for me. She expressed her feelings, and we both got married. Hence is why I referred to how my wife knows Meghana more than anyone else because they both are the same. Why do you think my daughter wants to be an English teacher and likes Shaktiman? She's a carbon copy of her mother. The 'Communication' and the 'Chemistry' worked for us.

All of us then went and watched Shaktiman together.

Moral of the Story: If you love a person, go and express it. Let's handle what happens later. Not everyone gets as lucky as Vardhan.

11

Har Ek Friend Zaroori Hota Hain!

10:42 PM, 03rd Mar 2023, Friday, Chennai, clicked sent on the final e-mail: It's been tough few weeks at work and with all the recession rumors spreading around; it looked like I'm on the edge of being fired. And just as I thought, I received a call from my boss and she told me, *"Chakri! I am sorry to be telling you this, but you are next in line for firing. I tried my best to delay it. I wanted to inform you so that you can start looking for other opportunities."*

Not her fault though, just that it had to happen. Anyway, just after the polite heads-up about being fired, I cut the call and texted a close friend of mine who works in a startup *"Bhai! I am getting laid off. Let me know if any openings are there in your firm"* and kept the phone aside. I lay down to take a nap, and in a few seconds, I received a reply, *"What! Let me check. As of now, it's very tight here as it is the time of promotions and hikes. Hence, the budget is little. But give me an hour to figure it out."* I acknowledged it and continued lying down on the bed.

11:30 PM, Same day, WhatsApp Notification from 'Police Station Joseph': Don't worry; he's the same friend I texted an hour ago. Wondering why his name is saved so? You need to time travel with me to 2012 to understand.

10: 30 PM, some day of some month in 2012, 1ˢᵗ year of Graduation, Nilgiri Hostel, Corridor notice board: There were times I forgot to take bath, but there were never when it comes to reading what was written on the notice board. The reason was, whenever Rasgullas were made in the hostel, we were informed through the notice board. And I never wanted to miss it. But that day, I saw a note which read, *'Strategy Meeting, 11:00 PM, Back Yard. Important (From Sandeep)'.* Sometimes, we used notice boards to share such critical information as well. It was a well-known fact that if the note was from Sandeep, there was a fight either in the last few hours, or a fight was planned in the next few hours, or sometimes both.

I was in dilemma on whether to attend it as I had a strategy presentation on *'Relationship Management'* in the first-hour post lunch for the next day and I didn't even prepare a slide by then. So, I strategized for 15 minutes, went to my room, wore my shoes, and ran straight to the backyard. While running, I watched YouTube videos on *'How to make presentations in 15 minutes.'*

11: 00 PM, Same Day, Hostel Backyard, 20 clueless people just like me, a confident Sandeep in the middle and a not-so-happy Pratik standing by his side: We had a full house from our wing. If we showed half of the interest in academics, we would have doubled our CGPAs. So, we were ready to see what it was all about. Breaking the developing curiosity, Sandeep pointed to Pratik and said, *"He picked up a fight with Joseph from CSE during the football match. The referee interrupted and sent them out of the field. After being sent out, they both agreed to complete the* *brawl interrupted by the referee at our hostel backyard at 11:30 PM. It is time we show what we are. Night watch starts now.*" Most of us were motivated by what Sandeep said but I was clueless. I barely knew Pratik. All that I know was, he was from my hostel, and I never interacted much with him. And, Joseph, I knew him a little as we both had a course in common. So, Pratik was more of a stranger to me than Joseph and I was going to fight for Pratik. *'Sometimes, you cannot fight by choosing sides; all that you can do is fight for what has already been chosen for you.'* And all of them thought I was good at strategizing and within no time I was handed over the responsibility to plan. I used all my brain, and made a foolproof plan for the fight.

My plan was to pick up cricket bats and form a 'V' shape and wait for them to come. I, Sandeep, and Pratik were in the first row. Sandeep as he likes to fight. Pratik as he got hit, and me, because I made the strategy. God knew what I was doing back then.

11:30 PM, Same Day, Hostel Backyard, Light Drizzles: Just as the time was 11:30 PM, we saw a bunch of guys running towards us. I was impressed by their punctuality. Only as they got closer, we saw hockey sticks in their hands. I was impressed by their preparation.

11:45 PM, Same Day, Hostel Backyard, Heavy Showers: It only took 15 minutes for me to get hit badly and, I was thrown away to the corner. In that second, I realized two things.

1. I was bad at strategy

2. Hockey Sticks are stronger than Cricket bats.

With all the energy I had, I stood up and jumped into the huddle again to get hit.

11:55 PM, Same Day, Hostel Backyard, *Showers Stopped*: I saw around 10 policemen running towards us. We even have a police station on campus, and someone informed them. And, by midnight, it was all chaos. It was dark and none of us had clue who was beating who. I was sure to have hit a couple of folks from my hostel itself. It looked like, 50 people (20 on Pratik's side, 20 on Joseph's side, and 10 on the side of Law and Order) were fighting only to realize that the Police were dominating. With every second of domination from the police, my mates kept looking at me in hope. But I did not have a backup plan on how to escape from the police because I thought my strategy was foolproof.

12:10 AM, Next Day (Date Changes), Hostel Backyard: It only took 10 minutes for the police to control the situation. Then I realized, Lathi is much more powerful than hockey sticks. What would happen next? We were all taken to the police station on campus. They made us stand in one single line and I was 38th in the line followed by Pratik and Joseph. All of us were still furious about not completing the fight. If by chance, there was a power cut in the station, all of us had only one thing on our minds, pick the lathi up and continue the fight. **'Divided by branches, united by the fight.'**

12:25 AM, Same Day, Police Station, and College Campus: Unfortunately, there was no power cut. One by one, we were questioned about what the fight was all about.

I then remembered, no one bothered to ask what the fight was all about in the first place. We were just excited to fight with no background in the brawl. And none of the guys standing before me in the line knew the background of the fight. So, whosoever said No, the constable smacked them with the Lathi. Trust me; there is no scarier feeling than waiting to be beaten up. Finally, my turn came, and I told him, ***"Sir, I too don't know the problem, but we were trying for the solution."*** He liked my answer and patted me twice. The only problem was he did it on my cheeks with extreme force. But I was eager to listen on what the fight was all about from Pratik and Joseph. They both were in sync and responded, **"Sir, he abused me first."** I was shocked as now we don't even have clarity about who started it first. I looked at Sandeep in disbelief only to see him arguing with a constable to increase the fan speed.

01: 00 AM, Same Day, Police Station, and College Campus: There was only one cell and all 40 of us were locked in the same cell. We didn't fight for the first half of the night as none of us had any energy left, and we didn't even fight for the next half of the night, as the injuries started paining. The ones not bleeding did first aid to the ones bleeding. **'Divided by branches, united by Injuries.'** So, the entire night, we were locked up in the cell and by the next morning, all of us became incredibly good friends. Wondering how? All of us might have had different branches in college and might be from different hostels but we all had one thing in common i.e., putting our lives for our friends. I believe that was more than enough to help us get close. **'Divided by branches, united by Friendship.'**

11: 45 AM, Same Day, Police Station, and College Campus: With a warning, they let us go and we headed back to our respective hostels.

12:15 PM, Same Day, C-32, and Nilgiri Hostel: I realized about the presentation which I had to make. I would have to repeat the semester if I missed the presentation and my father would still be fine If he knows about me being locked up in the police station but will disown me if he gets to know about me repeating the semester.

One thing common with our presentation group was all of us were involved in the fight and were injured, and the only thing not common was the place of the injuries on our bodies. All we had was zero preparation, 30 minutes, and 5 injured people. We put all our brains and prepared an introduction and a 'Thank you' slide. Before we started preparing the main slide, we realized it was already 1:00 PM. So, we left the main slide blank and thought of talking extempore.

1:00 PM, Same Day, Seminar Hall, and College Campus: We entered the seminar hall with bandages. Everyone in the seminar looked at us as if we were returning from war. Within 5 minutes, all of them knew what happened.

1:45 PM, Same Day, Seminar Hall, College Campus, and Professor called our team's name (The Adventurers) aloud: After what we have gone through in the last 12 hours, I felt our team's name was appropriate. While going on to the stage, we prepared what to speak and by the time we entered the stage, we forgot everything. Standing there, we thought; as the topic was about relationship management, let us talk about the relationships developed over the last 12 hours and what we learned as a part of Relationship Management based on our experiences. And it went like this.

"People often talk about relationship management with partners and parents but today, we want to talk about relationship management specific to friendships. Friendship and Rules are very closely related. Friendship lets you break the rules and rules don't define friendship." Such an irony right, got beaten up, landed in the police station, got a warning from the police and we were talking about rules.

"When all of us were kids, we were under the umbrella of parental guidance and protection. With age, you meet people who change your lives, and you end up doing things that are not defined in the rule book. And we'll learn some priceless life skills through such great friends. Today, we will talk about such friendships.

1. Before meeting them, we would be shy to watch alcohol commercials with our parents, but all of us would've tasted our first sip of alcohol only because of a friend. I never knew what brands existed when I was a kid, but now I know who the brand ambassadors are for those brands of alcohol. I have experienced some of the greatest things in life only because of friendship. **'Friendship gives you great Experiences'**

2. I often closed my eyes whenever a scene of a fight comes up on the screen. And now, I landed up

in a police station for being involved in a fight. Before friendship, I was scared to approach a girl and express feelings. Now, post-meeting them, I am courageous enough to talk to the girl I like. All that we had to do is tell our friends about whom we liked, and they'll work harder than UPSC to set a date for us. *'Friendship teaches you Courage'*

3. Before friendship, I did not have the confidence to talk on stage even after full preparation. But now, even with bruises and under-prepared slides, we are here talking. *'Friendship gives you Confidence'*

4. When I was a kid, I was bad at money management and was always scared of running out of money, and now with so many friends I didn't get any better, but I didn't have to worry about me running out of money. Not that, I earn heavily, but I borrow heavily and do not have to worry about ruining relationships. *'Friendship teaches you not to worry'*

5. When I was a kid, I was scared to go to the washroom at 3 AM, and now fortunately, I have friends whom I can ring up at 3 AM if I'm messed up in my life. And all of us would reciprocate the same. *'Friendship helps you gain Trust'*

6. I feared failure and rejection in childhood. But now, I am not scared of failure and rejection. Not that I don't fail. But only because I have shoulders to lean on, ears to listen to, and hearts that care for me. *'Friendship helps you handle ups and downs'*

All you need to have in life is a few friends with whom you can laugh, cry, live, love, and die. In the world of 800 Crore, find 8 good friends, 4 to carry you to the grave and 4 to keep you alive in their memories once you're dead. So, that's our presentation on relationship management. Hope you liked it!"

The eyes which gave us weird looks were teary, and the seminar hall which was filled with spreading information about us was filled with applause.

The professor too stood up and told, *"I'd give you a 20/20"*. And, seeing by your injuries, he asked if hockey sticks were used. We were amazed and asked him how he knows. I thought to myself, *"Did we beat him up too?"* We gave the smallest of nods, and he replied, *"Wondering how I know? Friendships, fights, hockey sticks, and police stations haven't started yesterday. It's only the presentations that started yesterday. I too was a part of one of such incidents long back."*

4 years passed, and the bunch of 40 people from the night stayed together. Joseph, Pratik and Sandeep were my best buddies.

11:47 PM, 03rd Mar 2023, Present Day: Now you know why I have a contact saved as *'Police Station Joseph'.* It was the same Joseph I fought against. The memories from the night of the brawl became weaker over time but the friendship with Joseph, Pratik, Sandeep and that bunch only became stronger. Oh, I did not reveal what Joseph replied right?

Joseph: *"Bhai! Have an interview scheduled for you on Friday. Same role with 20% hike."*

The man who told me how tough it was an hour back has got me an interview scheduled. Considering how short they were on a budget, I asked him several times how he was able to get it done. He didn't respond and asked me to concentrate on the interview.

11:00 AM, 06th **Mar 2023, Monday, Interview:** The interviewer was very friendly and kept on saying how highly Joseph spoke about me and finally, the HR offered me a job. I thanked him for hiring me despite them having budget constraints. The interviewer laughed and replied, *"Oh thank Joseph. He denied hike and promotion for himself creating an extra space on the budget with which we were able to hire you."*

I thanked the interviewer with a teary eye and left the room. Joseph greeted me outside the room and asked me how it went. I replied, *"It went awesome"*. He was more excited than and I waited to see if he would disclose what he has done for me. With my pause, I was sure, he figured out about me knowing it. He broke the pause with a hug and took me to a restaurant for lunch.

I then realized how lucky I am to have this bunch and Joseph as friends. If not for this guy, I would have been jobless. Who would have imagined, the person I met in the biggest fight of my life keeps fighting for me in all my fights of life ever since? I was glad to have fought with him that day. I might not have been lucky to have the brains to be good at academics, but I realized I was lucky to have had such good friends around me. I'd carry the scars of the fight and care for these guys for the life.

Moral of the Story: At any age of life, if you have few good friends on whom you can fall, you are rich, lucky, and blessed. Cheers to all the great friends and friendships.

Thank you for being patient and tolerant both with me and the book. Hope it gave you some good time.

Merci, Danke, Toda, Efharisto, Grazie, Arigato and Asante. Don't worry, they aren't wrongly spelt. They are just words for Thank you in various languages.

I would feel grateful if you can let me know your feedback about the book. It will help me with further attempts (hopefully). You can reach out to me on Flying__Saucerrr (Instagram) or Sai Ruthvik Rachakonda (LinkedIn, Facebook) for any feedback. Would love to hear and learn from you. It's been a great journey. Hope, it wasn't bad for you.

"Sapne har baar hamaare hi poora hona zaruri nahi hai, kabhi dusro ka bhi poora kar sakthe hai." My dream was to write a book and hope people read it. Thanks for fulfilling my dream!

www.ingramcontent.com/pod-product-compliance
Lightning Source LLC
Chambersburg PA
CBHW022052150726
47990CB00003B/1059